Mud

MARY LYN RAY

Illustrated by Lauren Stringer

VOYAGER BOOKS
HARCOURT, INC.
Orlando Austin New York San Diego Toronto London

Special thanks to Debra Frasier and Matthew Smith,
who were always there to give me a push
whenever I got stuck in the mud
—L. S.

Requests for permission to make copies of any part of the work should be
submitted online at www.harcourt.com/contact or mailed to the
following address: Permissions Department, Harcourt, Inc.,
6277 Sea Harbor Drive, Orlando, Florida 32887-6777.

www.HarcourtBooks.com

First Voyager Books edition 2001
Voyager Books is a trademark of Harcourt, Inc.,
registered in the United States of America and/or other jurisdictions.

The Library of Congress has cataloged the hardcover edition as follows:
Ray, Mary Lyn.
Mud/Mary Lyn Ray; illustrated by Lauren Stringer.
p.   cm.
Summary: As winter melts into spring, the frozen
earth turns into magnificent mud.
[1. Spring—Fiction.   2. Mud—Fiction.]
I. Stringer, Lauren, ill.   II. Title.
PZ7.R210154Mu   1996
[E]—dc20   94-28711
ISBN 978-0-15-256263-2
ISBN 978-0-15-202461-1 pb

K M O P N L

The paintings in this book were done in Lascaux acrylics
on Fabriano 140 lb. watercolor paper.
The display type was set in Poppl Exquisit.
The text type was set in Cloister
by Thompson Type, San Diego, California.
Color separations by Bright Arts, Ltd., Singapore
Printed and bound by Tien Wah Press, Singapore
Production supervision by Sandra Grebenar and Pascha Gerlinger
Designed by Lisa Peters

For Jed, who knows about mud

— M. L. R.

For Ruby and her toes

— L. S.

One night it happens.

Maybe it begins in the warm
of the day, and night only
releases the scent.

But it's always at night that it happens.

Someone opening
a door will notice:
earth comes unfrozen.

A cold sweet smell rises
in the ground, like sap
in the snow.

By morning brown leaves loosen
from their frozen drifts and run
rattling in the flapping wind.

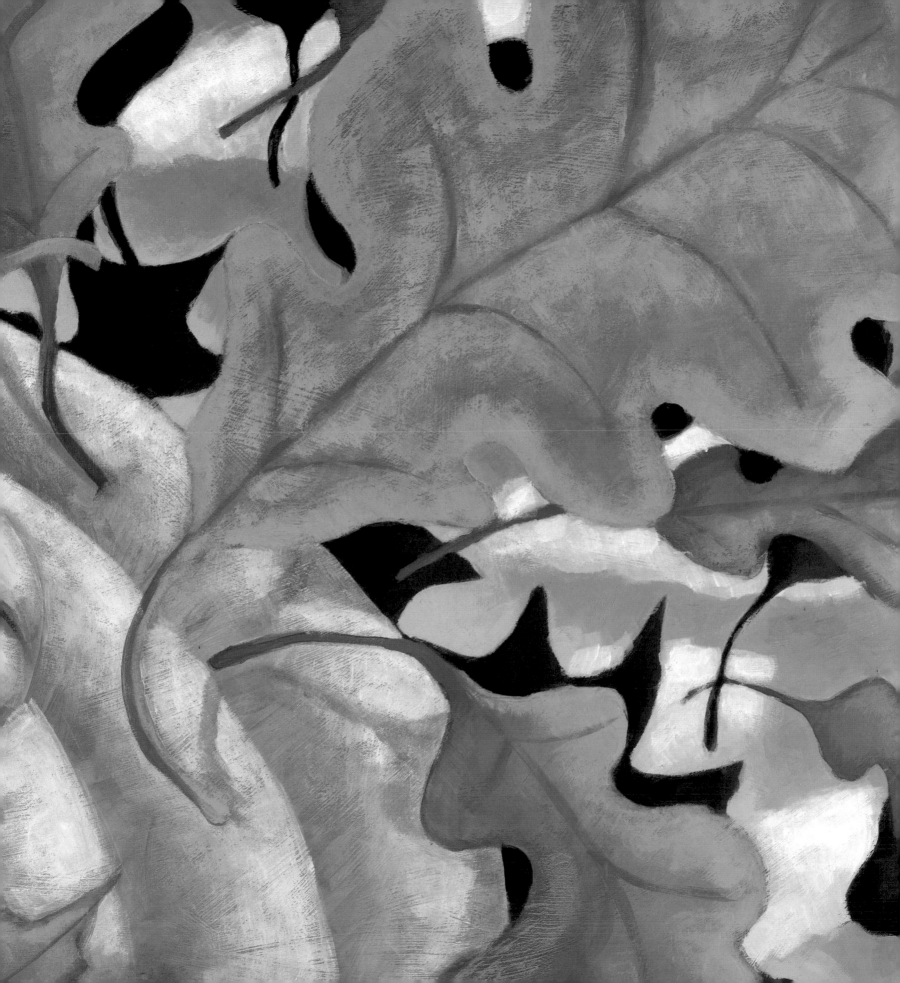

Small scattered stones,
where the sun has seen
them, will thaw pools
of grass.

The hills will remember their colors.

Happy mud.

Stir it. Stick it.

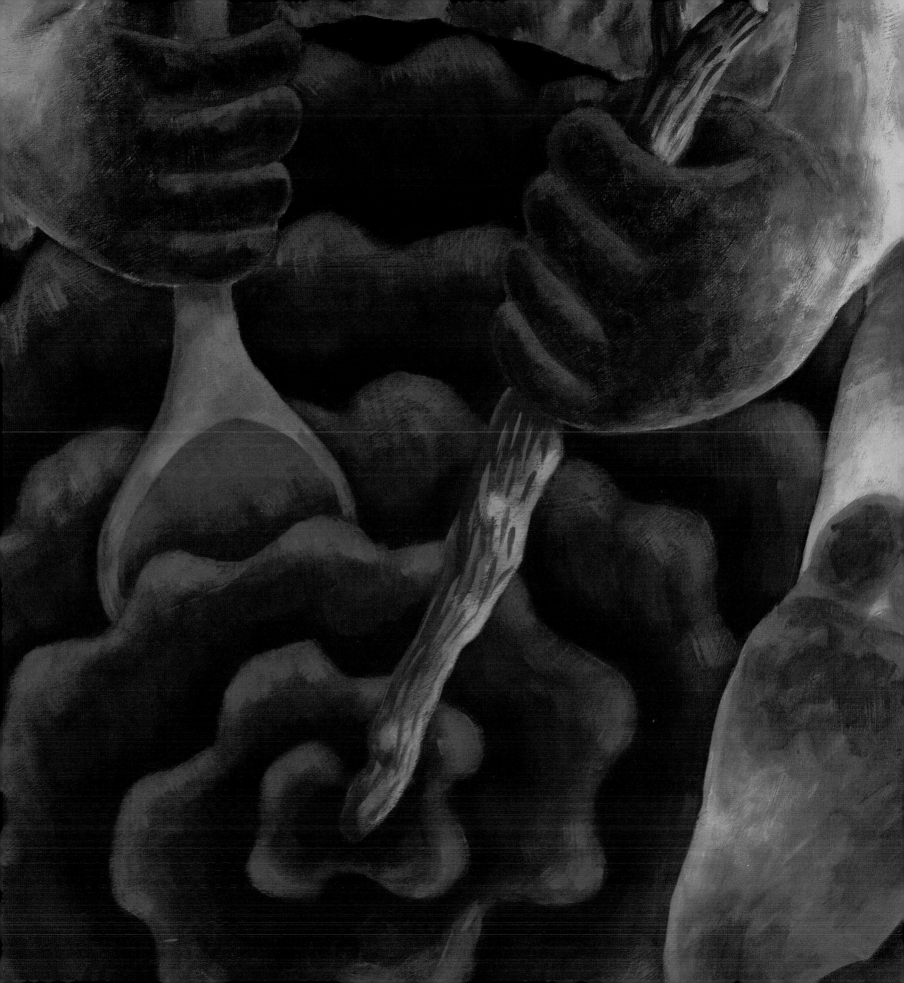

Dig it. Dance it.

Gooey, gloppy, mucky,
magnificent mud.

Come spring.
Come grass.

Come green.